One More Pet

Eugenie Fernandes

SCHOLASTIC CANADA LTD.

New York Toronto London Auckland Sydney
Mexico City New Delhi Hong Kong Buenos Aires

For Marvin and Betsy, and the Bird Lady.

> If you find an orphaned or injured animal, contact
> your local humane society or wildlife centre.

Scholastic Canada Ltd.
175 Hillmount Road, Markham, Ontario L6C 1Z7, Canada

Scholastic Inc.
555 Broadway, New York, NY 10012, USA

Scholastic Australia Pty Limited
PO Box 579, Gosford, NSW 2250, Australia

Scholastic New Zealand Limited
Private Bag 94407, Greenmount, Auckland, New Zealand

Scholastic Ltd.
Villiers House, Clarendon Avenue, Leamington Spa,
Warwickshire CV32 5PR, UK

The illustrations in this book were painted in gouache on Arches paper.
The type is set in 18 point Giovanni Book.

National Library of Canada Cataloguing in Publication Data

Fernandes, Eugenie, 1943-
One more pet

ISBN 0-439-98778-4
For children ages 4 to 8.

1. Pets —Juvenile fiction. I. Title.

PS8561.E7596O54 2002   jC813'.54   C2001-903337-0
PZ7.F363On 2002

6 5 4 3 2   Printed in Canada   02 03 04 05 06 07

This story is almost
entirely true.
It happened to me —
It could happen to you.

Once upon a summer day,
when Emily went out to play,
she found a skinny little cat
hiding in the shed. And *that*
is when she said, "Now, I can see,
this cat could use a friend like me."
She took it home and called it Cat —
and here's what happened after that.

She caught a wiggly pollywog.
At home it turned into a frog
with webby feet and googly eyes.
"I'll give you *lots* of dragonflies,
and slimy slugs to keep you fat
and happy, like my little cat."

When Emily ambled down the lane,
through puddles, in the pouring rain,
she found a rabbit, dripping wet.
And now she has another pet.

Her mother said, "You know, my dear,
it might begin to smell in here.
And what if they begin to leap
around your room when you're asleep?
You *really* have to think of that
with a rabbit, a frog and a little cat."

Then Alexander came to say,
"I have to give this rat away.
Although it's quiet as a mouse,
I cannot keep it at my house."

"A rat?" said Emily. "Okay.
I like rats. The rat can stay."
Now Emily has a lively rat,
a rabbit, a frog and a little cat.

When Emily went out to explore,
she found a duck down by the shore.
Her mother said it should go back,
but then the duck began to quack —
a melancholy sort of sound.
"I guess this one can stay around,"
her mother sighed. "But I don't think
I want to find it in the sink!"

"I don't want puddles everywhere.
I don't want feathers in my hair."

"Don't worry, Mom," said Emily.
"I'll keep it neat. Just wait and see."
Now Emily has a duck, a rat,
a rabbit, a frog and a little cat.

Then . . . at the shelter in the town,
Emily got a white and brown,
very cute and very spotted
little dog. And then she trotted
home and counted every spot.
There were a lot. And now she's got:
a spotted dog, a duck, a rat,
a rabbit, a frog and a little cat.

When Emily crawled beneath a bush
she was careful not to squoosh
a pretty little pea-green snake.
"I think that I would like to take
you home, where you will grow and shed.
I'll keep you underneath my bed.
Will Mother like this? We shall see.
Just look what's living here with me!
A snake, a dog, a duck, a rat,
A rabbit, a frog and a little cat!"

Then, walking through the woods, she found
a nest all broken on the ground,
with one small baby bird inside.
Its hungry mouth was open wide.
She fed it baby food and bugs.
She gave it tender-hearted hugs.
She taught it how to fly and sing.
She loved it more than anything.

Some people said it was absurd
to keep a noisy baby bird,
a snake, a dog, a duck, a rat,
a rabbit, a frog and a little cat.
But Emily kept them anyway
and she was happy. Then one day . . .

Emily heard somebody sneeze,
sniffle, snuffle, cough and wheeze!
The farmer wasn't feeling well,
so Emily said, "Now, I can tell,
you need someone to feed the lambs,
to milk the cows and brush the rams . . .

" . . . to gather eggs and find the goose,
and keep the goats from getting loose.
And clean the pigs, and catch the hen."
So Emily helped him out, and then . . .

When all the animals were fed,
Emily galloped home and said,
"Mother! Look! I have a horse."
"A *horse*?" cried Mother. "Yes, of course,"
said Emily. "I love her so."
But Mother said, "Good heavens, no!
We *really* haven't any place
to put a horse. There is no space."
Emily sighed. "This is not good."
But really, Emily understood.

So Emily took the horse away.
"My mother says it cannot stay."
"Gee, that's too bad," the farmer said.
"Here, take this giant egg instead.
It's rather large, but then, of course,
it's a *whole* lot smaller than a horse."

"It's wonderful!" cried Emily.
Then happily — and carefully —
she picked it up. "This egg will fit.
I will find a place for it.
I'm *sure* I will. I *know* I can.
So Emily took it home, and then . . .

She built a nest in Dad's old hat.
And what do you think happened after that?